Bright and Early Books

Bright and Early Books are an offspring of the world-famous Beginner Books® . . . designed for an even lower age group. Making ingenious use of humor, rhythm, and limited vocabulary, they will encourage even pre-schoolers to discover the delights of reading for themselves.

For other Bright and Early titles, see the back endpapers.

BRIGHT and EARLY BOOKS for BEGINNING Beginners

Hooper Humperdink...? NOT HIM!

Dr. Seuss's real name was Theodor Geisel.
On books he wrote to be illustrated by others,
he used the name Theo. LeSieg,
which is Geisel spelled backward.

3 1350 00255 3933

www.randomhouse.com/kids
www.seussville.com

Library of Congress Cataloging-in-Publication Data
LeSieg, Theo.
Hooper Humperdink—? Not him! / by Dr. Seuss writing as Theo. LeSieg ; illustrated by Scott Nash.
  p. cm. — (A bright & early book)
SUMMARY: A youngster plans a huge, spectacular party, inviting friends whose names begin with every letter from A to Z—except for one person.
ISBN 0-679-88129-8 (trade) — ISBN 0-679-98129-2 (lib. bdg.)
[1. Parties—Fiction. 2. Stories in rhyme. 3. Alphabet.] I. Nash, Scott, ill.
II. Title. III. Series.
PZ8.3.G276Hk 1997   [E]—dc20
96-001724

Printed in the United States of America First Edition 10 9 8 7 6 5 4 3 2 1
BRIGHT & EARLY BOOKS, RANDOM HOUSE, and the Random House colophon are registered trademarks of Random House, Inc. THE CAT IN THE HAT logo ® and © Dr. Seuss Enterprises, L.P. 1957, renewed 1986. All rights reserved.

Hooper Humperdink...? NOT HIM!

By Dr. Seuss*

*writing as Theo. LeSieg

Illustrated by Scott Nash

A Bright and Early Book
From BEGINNER BOOKS
A Division of Random House, Inc.

I'm going to have a party.
But I don't think
that I'll ask
Hooper Humperdink.

I'll ask Alice.

I'll ask Abe.

I'll ask Bob
and Bill
and Babe.

I'll ask Charlie, Clara, Cora.
Danny, Davey, Daisy, Dora.

I'll ask Dinny.
I'll ask Dot.

But Hooper Humperdink . . . ?
I'LL <u>NOT</u>!

Elma! Elly! Ethel! Ed!
Frieda, Francis, Frank and Fred.

I'll ask George and Gus and Gary.
Henry, Hedda, Hank and Harry!

I'll ask every kid I like.
Irene, Ivy, Izzy, Ike.
Joe and Jerry, Jack and Jim.

But Hooper Humperdink . . . ?
<u>NOT</u> <u>HIM</u>!

That Humperdink!
I don't know why,
but somehow
I don't like that guy.

A party needs
a band to play.

And so I'll get a band.
O.K.

The K. K. Kats
are on their way!

And I like
Lucy, Luke and Lum.
I like the Lesters.
<u>They</u> can come.

And Mark and Mary!
Mike and Mabel!
I'll have to get
a bigger table!

They'll come by air,
by parachute.

Nora,
Norton,
Nat
and Newt!

And Olivetta Oppenbeem!
I'll have to order more ice cream!

I'll need about ten tons,
I think.

But <u>none</u> for Hooper Humperdink!

No! Humperdink won't do at all.
He's not good fun
like Pete and Paul,
and Pinky, Pat and Pasternack.
I bet they come by camel back.

And so will
lots of other pals,
like the Perkins boys
and the Plimton gals!

Q . . . Q . . . Q . . .
Who begins with "Q"?
Quintuplets!

So I'll ask a few.

Ralph and Rudolf!
Ruth and Russ!

And some other R's
in a big blue bus.

Oh, what a party!
Sally! Sue!
Solly! Sonny!
Steve and Stoo!

I'll ask the Simpson sisters, too.

But
I'm not asking
<u>YOU</u> <u>KNOW</u> <u>WHO</u>!

Nobody
wants to play with Hooper.
Humperdink's a party-pooper!

Welcome, Tim and Tom and Ted!
Grab a hot dog. Get well fed.

Welcome, Ursula! Welcome, Ubb!
Strawberry soda by the tub!

Welcome, Vera!
Violet! Vinny!
Welcome, Wilbur, Waldo,
Winnie!

Xavier!
And Yancy! Yipper!
Zacharias!
Zeke and Zipper!

All my good friends from A to Z!
The biggest gang you'll ever see!
The biggest gang there'll ever be!

A party big and good as this
is too good for <u>anyone</u> to miss!

And so, you know,
  I sort of think . . .

. . . I <u>WILL</u> ask
Hooper Humperdink!

BRIGHT and EARLY BOOKS for BEGINNING Beginners

Other Bright and Early Books You Will Enjoy

by Stan & Jan Berenstain
HE BEAR, SHE BEAR
THE SPOOKY OLD TREE

by Marc Brown
WINGS ON THINGS

by Michael Frith
I'LL TEACH MY DOG 100 WORDS

by Al Perkins
HAND, HAND, FINGERS, THUMB
THE NOSE BOOK

by Richard Scarry
CHUCKLE WITH HUCKLE!

by Dr. Seuss
THE EYE BOOK
THE FOOT BOOK
THE TOOTH BOOK